Be a Camouflage Detective

Looking for Critters That are Hidden, Concealed, or Covered

Text and Artwork by
Peggy Kochanoff

NIMBUS
PUBLISHING
NIMBUS.CA

Nimbus Publishing Limited
3660 Strawberry Hill Street, Halifax, NS, B3K 5A9
(902) 455-4286 nimbus.ca

Printed and bound in Canada

NB1585

Design: Jenn Embree
Editor: Emily MacKinnon

Library and Archives Canada Cataloguing in Publication

Title: Be a camouflage detective : looking for critters that are hidden, concealed, or covered / Peggy Kochanoff.
Names: Kochanoff, Peggy, 1943- author, illustrator.
Description: Series statement: Be a nature detective series | Includes bibliographical references.
Identifiers: Canadiana (print) 20210215550 | Canadiana (ebook) 20210215615 | ISBN 9781774710005 (softcover) | ISBN 9781774710012 (EPUB)
Subjects: LCSH: Camouflage (Biology)—Juvenile literature. | LCSH: Protective coloration (Biology)—Juvenile literature. | LCSH: Animals—Color—Juvenile literature.
Classification: LCC QL767 .K63 2021 | DDC j591.47/2—dc23

Nimbus Publishing acknowledges the financial support for its publishing activities from the Government of Canada, the Canada Council for the Arts, and from the Province of Nova Scotia. We are pleased to work in partnership with the Province of Nova Scotia to develop and promote our creative industries for the benefit of all Nova Scotians.

Dedicated to my family (Stan, Tom, Jim, Avai, and Jaya) for all their wonderful support.

Many thanks to Jim Wolford (retired biology teacher at Acadia University) for checking my nature facts and wording.

Thanks also to Nimbus Publishing for all their help and encouragement, and for making the process fun.

Camouflage is a way for animals to blend into their surroundings and avoid being eaten by **predators**. It also helps animals that are hunting to sneak up on their **prey**.

Sometimes they mimic something (like a leaf or twig), or they might alter their appearance to match the colour of their hiding place (like a tree trunk). Some animals completely cover themselves with natural materials (like a flounder under the sand), while others startle or confuse an attacker (like the Io moth with "eyes" on its wings). If the camouflaged animals survive, they pass these **adaptations** on to their offspring.

Let's look closer at some wonderful camouflage methods!

See if you can guess all the animals hiding on the book's cover, and turn to page 51 to see if you guessed correctly.

Look up definitions to words in **bold** in the glossary at the back of the book, starting on page 52.

4

How are
ocean animals
camouflaged?

Hmmm…Let's look
closely and find out.

squid

sand dollars

sea anemone

hermit crab

moon snail

flounder

Sand Dollar

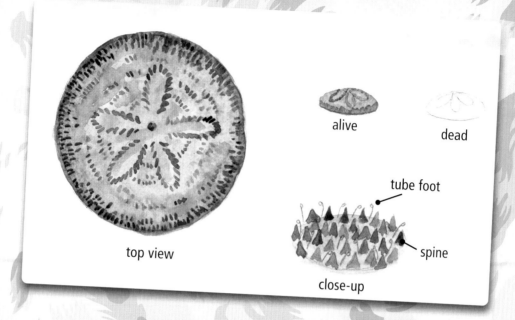

alive

dead

top view

tube foot

spine

close-up

This animal gets its name because it looks like an old silver dollar coin. Its colour ranges from purple to reddish-brown, and it only turns white once it dies. The surface of a sand dollar is covered in velvety spines and tiny tube feet. These feet help the sand dollars bury themselves in the sand when threatened or disturbed, so they become completely camouflaged. Besides helping with movement, the spines and feet also move food (algae, **crustacean larvae**, small **copepods**) to a mouth on the bottom of the urchin. The mouth has five teeth that may take fifteen minutes to grind food so it can be swallowed.

Because of its hard skeleton, the sand dollar has few predators. Once it dies and turns white, its spines disintegrate. The five teeth loosen, so if you shake a white sand dollar you can hear a rattle.

7

Moon Snail

shell

foot

Moon snails are a species of large predatory sea snails. Moon snails have a "gushy" foot that oozes slime. The foot moves the snail along the ocean floor and also pulls it under the sand so it is completely camouflaged. This is a wonderful way to hide from predators, but is also great for sneaking up on prey. Once the snail spies a clam, the foot engulfs it. Then a toothed structure (**radula**) drills a hole right through the clamshell! Its tubular mouth is inserted and sucks out the clam body. Yum!

sand collar

When a female moon snail is ready to lay eggs, she makes a layer of sand around herself stuck together with mucus. She then lays thousands of eggs between herself and the sand. A second layer of sand on top sandwiches the eggs and keeps them safe. When leaving the rubbery circle, the mama snail cuts an opening, forming a "collar." Eggs hatch in a few weeks and leave the collar behind, which then hardens and disintegrates.

If you find a moon snail's sand collar on the beach, you can touch it, but you must be gentle with it! If the collar is rubbery, it means it has live eggs inside, so pick it up carefully and return it to the water.

Sea Anemone

closed-up sea anemones

At first glance you might think sea anemones are plants, but they are actually very pretty animals! They live attached to a solid surface like a wharf, reef, or sea bottom. Their tentacles wave in the currents, waiting for small fish to swim by. The tentacles have stinging cells that shoot out and inject prey with a **neurotoxin**, which paralyzes them. Nearby tentacles hold the prey until it stills, then move it to the mouth, where the anemone swallows it whole. Their stomach **enzymes** are so strong that a small crab can be digested in five minutes! Non-digestible parts, such as bones and shells, are spit out.

When the anemone is disturbed or scared, the tentacles fold inward and it looks a bit like a wrinkled blob of jelly. This is wonderful camouflage as well as protection during low tide, when hungry birds are flying around overhead. Sea anemones can move position very slightly from day to day on their foot.

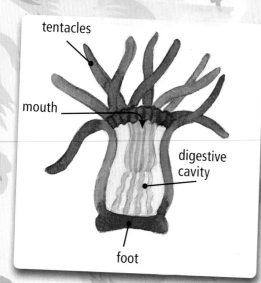

tentacles

mouth

digestive cavity

foot

10

Squid

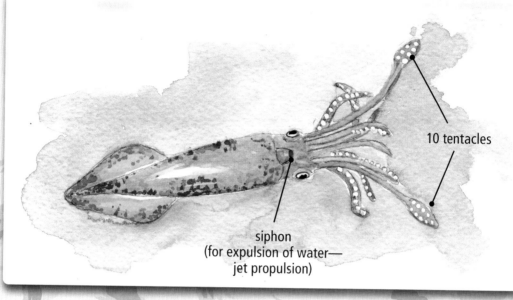

10 tentacles

siphon
(for expulsion of water—
jet propulsion)

These elongated creatures are graceful swimmers, and are also masters of camouflage. If threatened, squid release clouds of black ink into the water. Not only does the ink conceal them, giving them time to escape, but the ink can also freeze sensory receptors on the predator, which stuns them for a moment or two. By ejecting a stream of water from their siphon, they dart backward or forward to chase small fish and crustaceans.

Squid can change colours because their cells are full of **pigment**. When the pigment expands, more colour is visible. Squid are truly amazing at hiding: they can control their colour and match patterns of the sea floor, rocks, and reefs. Sometimes these colour changes occur when the animal feels stressed or threatened. They also have amazing eyes that are almost as complex as human eyes, which helps them keep a lookout for predators.

squid egg cases

Flounder

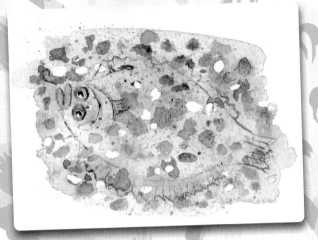

Like most fish, flounder start out with one eye on each side of their body. But after one month, flounder become "flat": one eye slowly moves to the other side, the mouth twists up, the lower side loses pigment and turns pale. Amazing! Now with both eyes on top, they can search for predators while looking for food (crabs, **invertebrates**, sea worms) along the ocean bottom.

Flounder are experts at camouflage. They have many pigmented cells on their upper side. When light hits their eyes, it is carried by nerves to these cells. The cells expand and contract, and are able to create different colours and textures to match the flounder's skin to pebbles, sand, mud, or even a checkerboard! By stirring the sand on the ocean floor, they can cover themselves and almost disappear before your eyes.

early flounder   flounder after eye migration

Hermit Crab

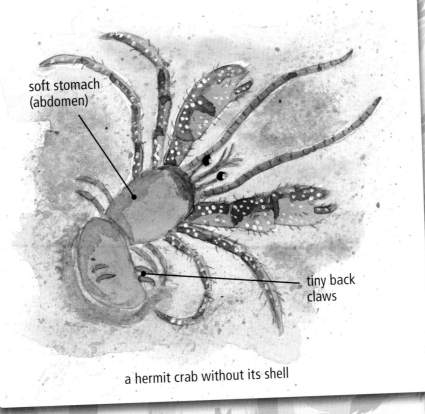

soft stomach (abdomen)

tiny back claws

a hermit crab without its shell

These funny little creatures can easily hide themselves in the shells of other animals. Unlike crabs with hard **exoskeletons** that split as they grow, hermit crabs have a soft belly, or **abdomen**, that needs protection. They look for empty shells (from whelk or moon snails) and use them to make a home. As hermit crabs grow, they abandon their current homes and go in search of larger shells. When they're ready to move out, tiny claws at the end of the abdomen unclasp. The hermit crab wiggles out, and then backs into the new home, where the tiny claws once again clasp the inside of the shell.

a hermit crab with its shell

a hermit crab with its shell

ordinary crab

If competition is great, hermit crabs may be fight each other over prime shell homes.

Once it pulls itself inside and blocks the shell opening with its claw, the hermit crab is hard to see. Sometimes it will even put a sea anemone or sponge on top of the shell, further camouflaging itself. A female hermit crab develops and holds eggs inside of her shell, attached to her abdomen. Once hatched, larvae swim free.

Hermit crabs eat plankton, algae, seaweed, dead and decaying animals, other crabs, mussels, tube worms, and shrimp.

How are pond
and river animals
camouflaged?

Hmmm…Let's look
closely and find out.

female red-winged blackbird

nest

bittern

green frog

caddisfly larvae

Green Frog

mottles

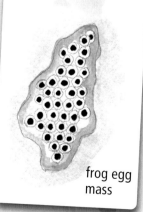

frog egg mass

This frog's colouring of green and brown blotches and **mottles** hides them well amongst the mud, algae, and rocks. A light-coloured belly camouflages them from predators in the water underneath looking up. Green frogs can also flatten their bodies among plants, rocks, and water surfaces, making them even harder to spot.

They eat insects, fish, crayfish, snails, spiders, small snakes, other frogs, and tadpoles.

Listen for their call, which is distinctive and sounds like a loose banjo string being plucked: *glunk*. Green frogs lay their eggs in a flat floating raft of jelly on the pond's surface.

While frogs are usually in or near water, toads can be found far from water, except when breeding. Unlike toads, they do not secrete a milky toxin.

17

Caddisfly

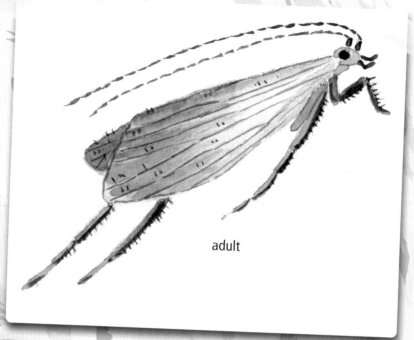

adult

Caddisfly larvae are perfectly camouflaged by hiding in tubes they build. Spun silk binds pebbles, sand, shells, twigs, leaves, or seeds into elongated tubes. The weight of these materials keeps the tubes on the pond floor. Both ends are open so oxygen-rich water flows in the back end, over the gills of the larva, and out the front, which allows them to breathe. Tiny hooks at the end of the larva's body hold it inside the tube while its head and legs can stick out the front.

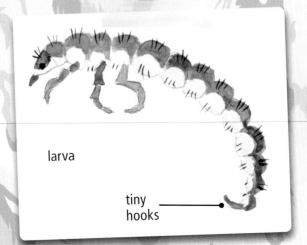

larva

tiny hooks

18

variety of larvae tubes (houses)

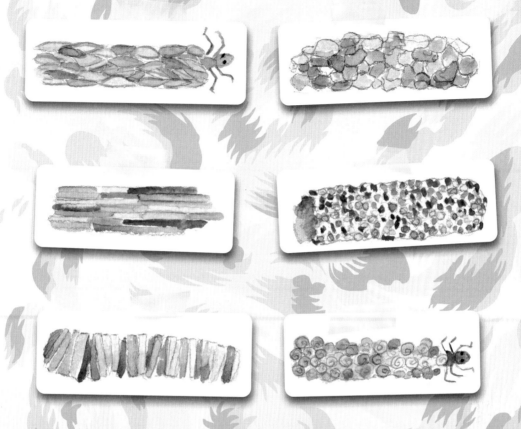

In late spring or early summer, larvae attach the tubes to the pond floor and plug the ends. Inside, over a period of two to three weeks, a **pupa** develops. Now an adult, the caddisfly emerges from the tube and swims to the surface. Living only a few weeks, they don't eat. They just mate, lay eggs, and die. Adult caddiflies are also important food for bats, birds, fish, lizards, frogs, spiders, and dragonflies.

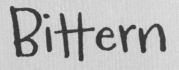

Bittern

bittern when not in a camouflage position

Bitterns are large marsh birds from the heron family. Their feathers are light brown and white, streaked with darker brown vertical stripes. When this bird stretches its long neck and bill upward, the stripes help it blend into grasses and reeds around ponds and rivers. It even sways back and forth with the wind like reeds do, perfectly camouflaged.

Living in marshes among reeds, bitterns look for fish, amphibians, crustaceans, and small mammals. Standing motionless, it can strike with lightning speed once it spots its prey. If you hear its call, you won't forget it. It sounds like a loud *boom* inside a metal oil drum. Noisy!

Red-winged Blackbird

female

nest in reeds

The female red-winged blackbird is neither red nor black! It is heavily streaked with brown stripes that help it blend in with grasses, reeds, and cattails, making it difficult for predators like hawks and owls to catch it, or see it building its nest or sitting on eggs. Females weave basket-like nests between reeds and cattails and line them with soft grass, so not only is the mother bird camouflaged, but her eggs are too!

male (larger
in size than
female)

The male is just the opposite with glossy black feathers and beautiful red-and-yellow shoulder patches (which can puff out). He wants to be seen to attract females, and to scare off rival males.

The main diet of red-winged blackbirds is seeds, but they also like to eat berries, fruit, snails, spiders, millipedes, and other insects.

How are animals camouflaged in the woods?

Hmmm...Let's look closely and find out.

grey squirrel

barred owl

woodcock

garter snake

baby white-tailed deer

toad

Toad

toad eggs in strings

A toad's skin varies in shades of green, brown, yellow, and black that blends in perfectly with dead leaves and grass. That, together with bumps and spots, keeps them well hidden from predators. They also have other ways of camouflaging: they are able to keep perfectly still, so they may not be seen, and they can even play dead. Toads can also bury themselves in the soft ground and disappear before your eyes. Adult toads live in moist, open habitats such as fields and backyards.

When threatened, toads produce a milky substance that oozes from a big gland behind the eye. This toxin kills small animals, can make your dog sick, and may cause allergic reactions in people, and if you pick one up, it may pee on you. So wash your hands after handling toads!

Toads vs. Frogs

TOADS	FROGS
• Skin is dry, thick, and bumpy.	• Skin is smooth and wet, and needs to be near or in water.
• Short legs help them make small hops.	• Long legs help them jump far.
• Eggs are laid in strings covered in jelly.	• Eggs are laid in clumps covered in jelly.

25

Grey Squirrel

Grey squirrels have two different fur-colour phases that help them camouflage. The black phase is more common in northern areas where there is a lot of shade to hide in. It also may be more common due to the colder weather up north, as black fur allows animals to better absorb heat. The lighter grey phase is produced by lead-grey **underfur**, plus "guard hairs" that are grey, or black tipped with white.

Grey squirrels often sneak up tree trunks headfirst out of sight or stand motionless, also making them hard to see. Their marvellous tail helps them steer while jumping from tree to tree. It also shades them from the sun, warms them up when cold, and distracts predators. A grey squirrel's favourite food is nuts but they also eat seeds, flower buds, flowers, insects, bird eggs, frogs, and mushrooms.

26

Fawn

Sweet little white-tailed deer babies (called fawns) are born with red-brown fur that is covered in white spots. These spots help the babies blend into the forest floor, which is often dappled with sun and shade. Fawns have no scent and when motionless, they are nearly invisible to predators. For the first few days of a fawn's life, its mother leaves for long periods of time to feed herself. But don't worry! She returns so the baby can nurse. So if you should find a fawn all alone, don't assume it is an orphan. After a few days they grow strong enough to follow their mother. By the fawn's first winter (90–120 days old) they lose their spots, and their coat turns greyish. Adult deer can stand very still so you can't see them until they move. In summer their coat is reddish-brown, while in winter it is grey-brown. When old enough, fawns eat grass, twigs, leaves, nuts, fruit, lichens, and corn. They are eaten by coyotes, bears, cougars, bobcats.

Garter Snake

Garter snakes have many colour patterns, but most commonly have three lighter stripes on a body of brown, black, grey, or olive-green. The lighter stripes make it difficult to tell which direction the snake is moving and how fast it is going. Some garter snakes have blotches and spots, which helps camouflage them among leaves, dirt, and rocks.

Garter snakes are harmless to humans, as they aren't venomous and they don't constrict (squeeze). But just be careful: if you do pick one up, it may squirt a stinky fluid on you. Look for them in the daytime in warmer months. During winter, they hibernate together in large groups to ensure they stay at a minimum temperature for survival.

When garter snakes grab their prey, they swallow it whole—sometimes while it's still alive! They eat slugs, snails, worms, insects, amphibians, leeches, fish, and other snakes.

Woodcock

A woodcock is a plump, short-legged **shorebird**. Its feathers vary in colour and markings from brown to yellow to orange or black, and this makes it resemble the leaf litter in which it hides and builds its nests. Like some of the other woodland animals we've met, the woodcock will also sit motionless so a nearby predator won't see it.

A woodcock uses its long and flexible beak to poke the soil for wiggly earthworms (its favourite food). It also likes to eat insect larvae, ants, snails, seeds, and some vegetable matter. With eyes set far back on its head, a woodcock can watch for predators above and behind while it's eating.

The male is famous for its "sky dance." At dusk, it flutters in upward spirals while the wind on its flight feathers creates a twittering sound. The spirals get smaller and smaller until he tumbles to the ground where he makes a nasal *neap* sound.

Barred Owl

This type of owl has beautiful feathers with a pattern of light and dark (called "mottled barring") which blends perfectly into the tree trunks where they like to perch. The feathers are barred vertically on the owl's abdomen, and horizontally on the owl's chest.

Barred owls are one of the best-camouflaged birds. They usually hunt at night, because they have excellent night vision along with super hearing. Their feathers have fluffy edges, which allow them to fly silently while hunting for rabbits, squirrels, chipmunks, mice, amphibians, reptiles, or small birds. Like all owls, they can't move their eyes in their sockets but turn their heads up to 270 degrees right and left to look for prey.

Listen for their call, which sounds like they're saying, "who cooks for you, who cooks for you all." If you hear it, try responding! They often call back.

mottled barred feathers

30

How are animals camouflaged in the snow?

Hmmm...Let's look carefully and find out.

snowy owl

short-tailed weasel
(winter colouration)

ptarmigan

snowshoe hare
(winter colouration)

Short-tailed Weasel

black-tipped tail

summer colouration

Short-tailed weasels are small **carnivorous** mammals. This weasel is also known as an ermine or a stoat. Its winter coat is white, thick, and soft, and hides it well in the snow. The black tip of a weasel's tail can be used to confuse predators. They will wave it so predators attack the tail instead of the body. Their long slender bodies help them hunt under the snow in burrows in wintertime, and among dense **vegetation** in warmer months. Their summer coat is brown on top and white underneath.

For such a small animal, they are fierce hunters and eat rodents, rabbits, birds, and bird eggs.

33

Snowshoe Hare

summer colouration

large fuzzy hind feet

Snowshoe hares are only found in North America and are one of its most common forest animals. As the seasons change and the days get shorter, a hare will shed its fur in a process called "molting." They grow new hair, and the tips of this new hair turn white, while the fur underneath is grey.

Hares versus rabbits

Although hares look a lot like rabbits, they are not the same! Hares are quite a bit bigger, with larger feet, and longer ears, legs, and bodies. Hares are also faster than rabbits, reaching speeds of up to 60 kilometres an hour! (A rabbit's top speed is around 29 kilometres an hour.) Baby hares are born with fur, open eyes, and the ability to hop around, while baby rabbits are born naked, with their eyes closed, and helpless.

rabbit   hare

This white fur is great camouflage in the snow—unless winter snows are late or melt early, making their white body stand out against the brown dirt and leaves.

The name "snowshoe" hare is given because these animals have large, furry hind feet, making it easier for them to move on top of snow.

In addition to changing the colour of their fur to blend in, the snowshoe hare's main defense is being able to sit perfectly still. If they do have to flee they can bound (up to three metres!) in all directions and reach speeds of up to 60 kilometres an hour.

Snowshoe hares eat a variety of plants, grasses, leaves from shrubs, and in winter, bark, twigs, and buds. They are eaten by lynx, coyotes, foxes, mink, hawks, and owls.

Snowy Owl

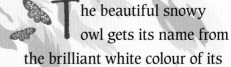

The beautiful snowy owl gets its name from the brilliant white colour of its feathers, which blend into the snow. The heaviest owl in North America, they weigh an average of four pounds. Their thick feathers, which even cover their legs and feet, keep them warm.

Male snowy owls only have a few dark flecks throughout their feathers, while females have many more. Juveniles (young owls) have lots of dark markings until they become whiter as adults.

Unlike most owls, snowy owls hunt during the day, when their bright white coat is less likely to stand out. Lemmings are their favorite food but they also eat deer mice, meadow voles, rats, hares, rabbits, muskrats, squirrels, geese, ducks, pheasants, gulls, and songbirds.

Like all owls, snowy owls can't move their eyes side to side (like people) but can move their head 270 degrees left or right.

feathered feet

36

Ptarmigan

summer colouration (female)

A small, ground-dwelling bird, the willow ptarmigan is a master of disguise. While its summer feathers are a mix of brown, red, and white, in the wintertime it molts to a bright white coat, starting with the head. When they first hatch, ptarmigans scurry along the ground like mice. However, within a week or so, they can fly (even if it's rather clumsy-looking!).

feathered feet

Each fall, the scales on the ptarmigan's feet give way to tiny bristly spines that nearly make each foot nearly double in size. This makes their weight more evenly distributed, which in turn makes it easier for the birds to navigate in snow.

The ptarmigan, however, has an extra level of winter protection: in addition to the spines, these birds sprout large foot feathers that act like snowshoes, increasing both surface area and warmth. In the spring, the spines and foot feathers fall off, and are replaced by scales once again.

At night, ptarmigans often burrow under the snow for shelter and camouflage. When discovered, the bird bursts out, spraying snow everywhere. They eat twigs, leaves, flower buds, seeds, berries, and some insects.

willow ptarmigan bursting from snow

38

How are insects camouflaged in the woods?

Hmm...Let's look closely and find out.

white admiral butterfly

io moth

katydid

treehopper

underwing moth

spittlebug

walking stick

crab spider

White Admiral Catterpillar

The caterpillar of the white admiral butterfly resembles bird poop, which is a wonderful example of camouflage—not many animals are interested in eating bird poop, so they get left alone. The caterpillars eat leaves from willow, cherry, aspen, poplar, cottonwood, and shad bush trees.

To survive winter, the caterpillar hides in a cut leaf folded up and attached to a branch with silk

chrysalis

41

adult white admiral

called a chrysalis. This, too, is excellent camouflage as the chrysalis just looks like a lonely dead leaf.

The adult white admiral butterfly emerges from the chrysalis around the middle of June. Adults drink liquid from animal dung, blooming or decaying flowers, tree sap, or rotting carcasses. Watch for them sunning themselves and slowly opening and closing their pretty black-and-white wings. They fly in short flights low to the ground.

Treehopper

Treehoppers are very difficult for predators to see—they are master hiders! These bugs have a bit that pokes straight up on the top of their head that looks like a thorn on a branch. They also avoid detection because they are so small and can hold very still. Giant leaps get them out of danger quickly.

For food, a treehopper pierces a tree branch and sucks the sap up with a straw-like mouthpart. Sugary **excretions** (called "honeydew") come out of the treehopper's back end and get licked up by ants. Females lay about sixty eggs at a time and protect them from intruders by waving their arms and kicking their back legs.

Crab Spider

This spider gets its name because as it can walk forward, backward, and sideways just like a crab. It also holds its front pair of legs like a crab. Instead of building webs like most spiders, crab spiders sit on flowers, waiting for insects to land where they can grab them. Over several days, a crab spider's colour can change to match different flowers (white, yellow, pink, green) so they blend in perfectly and insects don't notice them. Disguise and surprise!

The crab spider's fangs are small compared to other types of spiders, but the venom acts quickly and paralyzes their prey. Eight little eyes allow them to see in all directions.

eight eyes on a spider's head, which is changed to yellow

44

Io Moth

male

female

The beautiful Io moth has large eyespots on its hind wings. When it opens its wings, these eyes appear, with the white in the centre of the black spot mimicking light reflection. This scares potential predators, making them think a larger, big-eyed predator is in front of them. These eyespots also distract predators, so they aim for the moth's hind wings instead of its body.

Males are bright yellow and have larger antennae, while females are reddish-brown.

light reflection

45

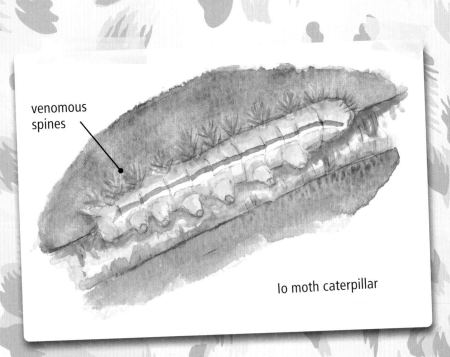

venomous spines

Io moth caterpillar

During the day, the dull, bland colouration of moths helps them blend into their surroundings and hide. There are six-and-a-half times more moths than butterflies, but they are so camouflaged and inactive during the day that you hardly notice them.

Adult Io moths have what's called a "vestigial mouthpart," which means a mouth that doesn't actually work, or sometimes no mouth at all! This means they don't eat, they just mate and lay eggs.

Be careful of touching the Io moth caterpillars because their spines are mildly venomous, which might cause irritation to your skin!

46

Underwing Moth

forewing

This moth's **forewing** is mottled with an irregular pattern of grey and brown, much like the colour and texture of tree bark. When resting on tree trunks, it is very difficult to see these moths. The better camouflaged they are, the more likely they will survive and pass this colouration on to offspring.

When the moth is disturbed, the **underwing** opens and flashes brightly coloured patterns (which only show when flight). Predators like bats and birds are startled and confused by this sudden flash of colour, so they usually attack the bright underwing instead of the vital body. Underwing moths (like most moths) are most active at night.

underwing

47

Spittlebug

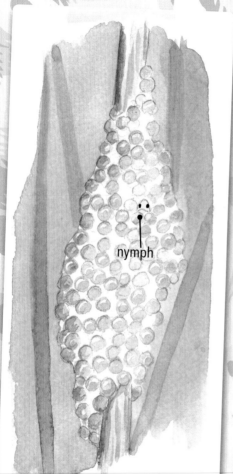

nymph

In the fall, a mother froghopper (spittlebug) lays her eggs in plant tissue. When the young (**nymph**) hatches from eggs in spring, it sucks juices from the plant where it was laid. As this liquid passes out of the spittlebug's back end, air is blown into it, making the liquid foamy. The nymph then hides inside the foam, completely camouflaging and protecting it from enemies. It is also protected from drying out from the sun, heat, and wind. Adults are called froghoppers because they leap from plant to plant, like a frog. They can jump one hundred times their body length!

Although these bugs are quite common, they occur in small numbers and cause little damage. Pesticides are not effective against themas nymphs are protected by their foam.

nymph
(spittlebug)

adult
(froghopper)

48

Katydid

ear

female katydid

The wings of these grasshopper-like insects mimic leaves in shape and colour, and even veins. This is lucky because they are poor fliers, which makes it difficult for them to escape from predators. Male katydids sing to attract females. The wing covers of a male have rasps and ridges (like a fiddle and bow) which, when rubbed together, produce their distinctive song that sounds like *katy-did*. Their ears are on the upper part of the front legs.

Since katydids are nocturnal and very good at blending into leafy surroundings, they are usually heard but not seen. They feed on flowers and leaves and are eaten by bats, birds, rodents, spiders, tree frogs.

Walking Stick

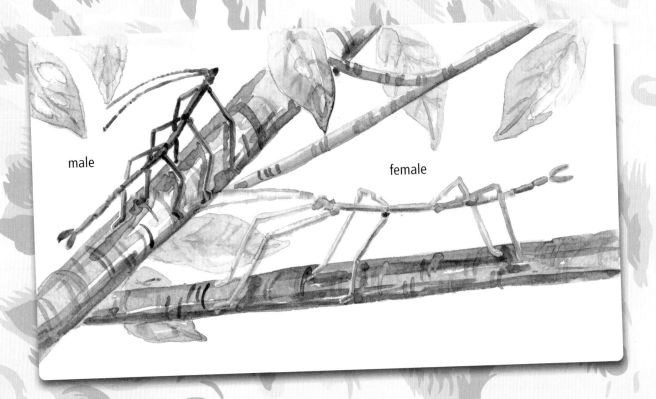

male

female

This insect has a wonderful type of camouflage. It is very thin and sits on tree branches so it resembles a twig. At rest, the first pair of a walking stick's legs extends forward between the antennae, making it look even more twig-like. The smaller male (75 mm) is brownish while the larger female (95 mm) is greenish-brown. There are over two thousand species of walking stick, and they eat a variety of plants like locusts, cherry, and walnut, but prefer oak and hazelnut. They feed on the tissue between veins on tree leaves. Because they have no wings, they move and disperse slowly, so if they weren't so good at camouflaging, they would be easy prey for birds, rodents, and spiders.

50

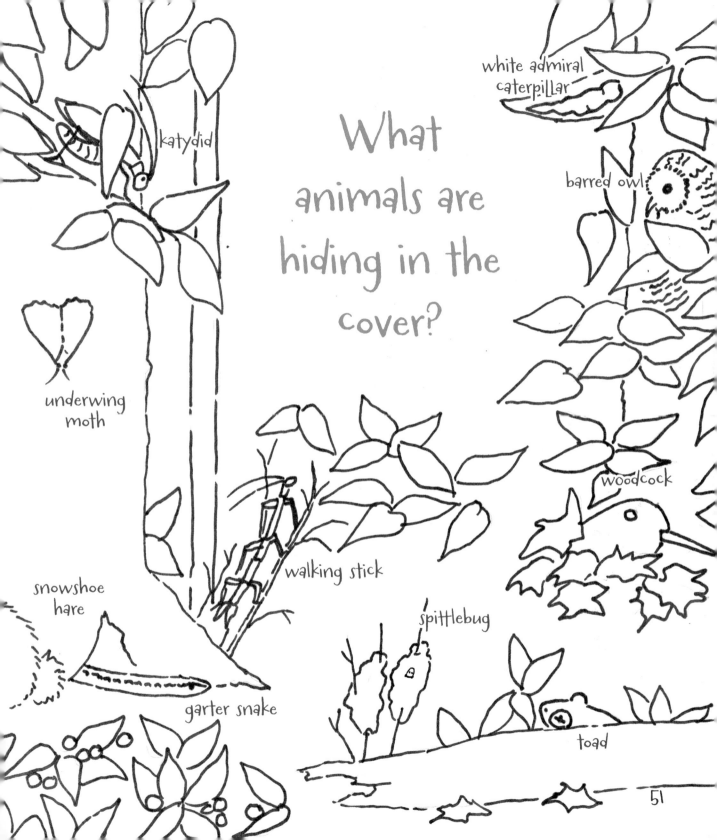

katydid

white admiral caterpillar

barred owl

What animals are hiding in the cover?

underwing moth

woodcock

walking stick

snowshoe hare

spittlebug

garter snake

toad

51

Glossary

abdomen: The part of the body containing the digestive organs. The belly.

adaptation: The process by which an animal or organism becomes more suited to its environment.

carnivorous: A plant or animal that feeds on animal tissue. A meat-eater.

copepod: Small or microscopic aquatic crustaceans.

crustacean: Aquatic arthropods (animals without backbones, and with segmented bodies, jointed appendages, and exoskeletons) including crabs, shrimp, and lobsters.

enzyme: A substance produced by an organism that starts (and increases) a chemical reaction.

excretion: Waste material that is eliminated.

exoskeleton: Rigid external covering that protects and supports.

forewing: Two front wings.

invertebrate: An animal that does not have a backbone.

larva (singular)/**larvae** (plural): Immature forms of an insect, such as a caterpillar.

mottles: An irregular pattern of spots or patches of colour.

neurotoxin: A poison that acts on the nervous system.

nymph: Immature form of an insect.

pigment: Natural colouring found in the tissue of plants and animals.

predator: An animal that hunts, kills, and eats other animals.

prey: An animal that is hunted and killed for food.

pupa: An insect in an immature form between larva and adult.

radula: In a mollusk, a tongue-like structure that scrapes food particles.

shorebird: Birds that nest along the shore, typically the ocean but also lakes and rivers.

underfur: An inner layer of short, fine fur providing warmth and waterproofing.

underwing: Hind wing of a moth usually hidden by the forewing.

vegetation: Plants in a particular area.